The Chocolate Monster

Jan Page

Illustrated by

Tony Ross

For My Father

Series Reading Consultant: Prue Goodwin
Reading and Language Information Centre,
University of Reading

THE CHOCOLATE MONSTER
A CORGI PUPS BOOK : 0 552 546046

First publication in Great Britain

PRINTING HISTORY
Corgi Pups edition published 1998

Set in 18/25pt Bembo Schoolbook by
Phoenix Typesetting, Ilkley, West Yorkshire.

Corgi Pups Books are published by Transworld Publishers Ltd,
61–63 Uxbridge Road, Ealing, London W5 5SA,
in Australia by Transworld Publishers (Australia) Pty. Ltd,
15–25 Helles Avenue, Moorebank, NSW 2170,
and in New Zealand by Transworld Publishers (NZ) Ltd,
3 William Pickering Drive, Albany, Auckland.

Made and printed in Great Britain by
Cox & Wyman Ltd, Reading, Berks.

Contents

Chapter One

Lucy was always losing things. She lost her glasses and her hairbands. She lost her library books, her gym pumps and her swimming towel. She lost the laces from her trainers and the

buttons from her coat. She lost the top of her drinking flask and the bottom of her recorder. And every time Lucy lost something Mum lost her temper.

"Why don't you look after things?" Mum would shout. "You would lose your head if it wasn't screwed on!"

"It's not my fault!" Lucy would reply. "I *don't* lose things. They just disappear!"

Lucy felt she was telling the truth. She always tried to keep her eyes on things. When she saw a button hanging off its thread she would tell herself to catch it and put it in her pocket.

But she never saw it fall! One minute it was there, the next it was gone.

And her glasses were *always* vanishing. One moment they were on her nose,

and the next – nowhere to be seen!

She had just lost her third pair of glasses that year, and it was only February.

"Where have you looked?"
asked Mum, really annoyed.

"Everywhere."

"You can't have looked *every-where*. Look in your school bag!"

Lucy looked in her school bag. She found three chocolate wrappers and a note she should have given to her mother last Wednesday, but her glasses weren't there.

"Look in your coat pockets!"
said Dad.

Lucy looked in her coat
pockets and found the key to her
bicycle padlock, which she had
lost the other week, but no
glasses.

"Lucy Locket lost her pocket!"
sang her brother Matthew.

"I haven't lost my pocket!
You *can't* lose a pocket!"

"*You* could!" replied Matthew,
dancing round the room. "Lucy
Locket! Lucy Locket!"

"Look in the sitting room,"
tried Mum.

But the glasses were not in the

sitting room – not down the side
of the sofa, not beside the video,
not under the television guide

and not under the rug.

"Look in the kitchen!" said
Dad.

Lucy knew her glasses were
not in the kitchen but she went
to look anyway. She pulled out
the washing machine and found
a dirty sock. She looked behind

the breadbin and found some
old cornflakes and three raisins.

Then she got down on her
tummy and peered under the
fridge. She found a fork, two
shrivelled peas and a fridge
magnet, but still no glasses.

"Why are you always losing
things?" shouted Dad crossly.
"Matthew never loses anything!"

Matthew gave a smug smile.
He followed Lucy from room
to room, chanting, "Lucy Locket
lost her pocket! Lucy Locket lost
her pocket!"

"I tell you they've disappeared!" Lucy said at last.

"No they haven't! Things don't just vanish into thin air!" cried Mum.

Mum was right. Things didn't just vanish into *thin air*. They

went somewhere. And Lucy
wished she knew exactly where
that somewhere was.

Chapter Two

After a few days Mum took
Lucy to the opticians to order
yet another new pair of glasses.
The optician was not very
pleased. Nor was Mum.

"Try wearing them round your neck on a chain," said the optician.

So Mum bought Lucy a gold chain and hooked the frame of her new glasses onto either end. When they weren't on her nose, the glasses sat on Lucy's chest where she could keep an eye on them.

And it seemed to work! For a whole month Lucy managed not to lose her glasses. From the moment she woke up she put the chain round her neck and she didn't take it off until she went to sleep.

"You look stupid! You look like a little old lady!" teased Matthew.

"Leave me alone!" cried Lucy.
"I bet you a whole week's
pocket money you lose those
glasses!"

Lucy went for Matthew, but
he skipped out of the way.

"Lucy Locket lost her pocket! Lucy Locket lost her pocket!" he teased.

Lucy chased him up the stairs and into the bedroom. She picked up her pillow and tried to bash him over the head. But Matthew leapt onto the bed and bounced out of her way, chanting his favourite rhyme.

"Lucy Locket lost her pocket!"

"Get lost! You're the most horrible brother in the world!"

Matthew jumped off the bed and ran off laughing. Lucy sat down and burst into tears.

Crying made her glasses steam up so she took them off and went to find a tissue.

She only left them for a moment, but a moment was all that was needed. When Lucy came back the glasses had vanished!

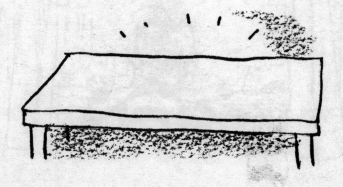

"Matthew!" she called out. "Give me my glasses back, I know you've got them!" But Matthew had gone into the garden to play football. He couldn't have taken the glasses. So where had they gone?

Lucy looked everywhere. She looked under her pillow and behind the curtain. She looked on the top of her wardrobe and in the bottom of her toy-box.

She emptied all her drawers and took off all the bedclothes. The room looked a terrible mess and she still hadn't found her glasses!

Then she spotted something shining on the carpet. It was the gold chain, poking out from under the bed. So that's where they were!

Lucy got down and crawled on her tummy. It was very dark

and dusty under there. She found
a ruler, an old vest and six felt
pens, but – no glasses!

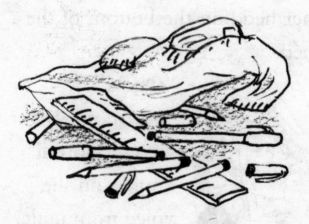

"Bother! Bother! Bother!" she
cried, banging her fist three
times on the floor.

"Come in!" said a voice. And
someone – or something – lifted
up a floorboard!

Chapter Three

Lucy was so shocked she banged her head on the bottom of the bed.

"Ouch!"

"Hurry up! I haven't got all day!" said the voice from under the floor.

Lucy shuffled forward and looked into the hole. It was very dark, but after a few seconds her eyes got used to the gloom. And then she could not believe what she was seeing! Sitting on a plastic box in the centre of what looked like a sitting room, was a small monster, about the size of a rabbit.

He was very peculiar to look at, rather fat and wrinkly, with several pairs of eyes and a head that was far too big for his tiny body. He was wearing a cloak covered in hundreds of buttons, and a small crown, which looked like the silver ring Lucy had lost on her birthday. He had odd

gloves on both his hands and feet, and he was wearing three pairs of Lucy's glasses!

"Excuse me, but everything you're wearing is mine!" said Lucy.

"Not any more," said the monster. "Finders keepers, losers weepers."

"That's not fair! I don't lose things — you have been stealing them!"

"Me a thief? How dare you?" replied the monster. "I only take what you leave lying around."

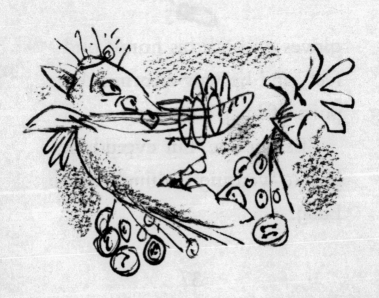

"But I only put those glasses
down for a second! Give them
back to me – right now!"

"Never! Finders, keepers –
that's the rule round here."

"Well, it's a very stupid rule,"
said Lucy crossly. "Who are you,
anyway?"

"I am the keeper of the Lost Property Cupboard. Every house has a Lost Property Cupboard, didn't you know?"

Lucy shook her head. "We have a Lost Property Cupboard at school, but they don't keep things for ever," she replied. "If you've lost something you can go to the Lost Property Cupboard and *get it back!*"

"Well, it doesn't work like that here. I put everything you lose to good use. And a rather splendid job I've made of this place, don't you think?"

Lucy looked around her. It *did* look warm and cosy, and there was something about the room that was rather familiar . . .

The room was lit by the
beam of a torch which stood in
the corner. And now she looked
closely, Lucy could see that the
walls were papered with letters
typed on white paper – school

letters! The chairs were plastic
lunchboxes and the table was a
stack of library books. There was
a vase made from the bottom of
a recorder and a camera which
sat in the corner like a television.

The carpet was bright and stripy with a picture of a fish. It was an old swimming towel! At the back of the room was the monster's bed. It had handkerchiefs for sheets and a great pile of hats and scarves for blankets. In fact,

everything in the room had once belonged to Lucy. Here were all the things she had ever lost in her life!

"Why do you only take *my* things?" she asked.

"Because I live under your bed, of course," replied the monster.

"That's not fair!" cried Lucy. "You keep getting me into trouble."

But the monster didn't seem to care too much about that.

"There's only one thing you look after properly. Only one thing you never, *never* leave lying around."

"Really?" said Lucy, surprised. "What's that?"

"The chocolate bars you buy with your pocket money." The

monster gave a huge, longing
sigh. "Oh, I so love chocolate!
Every time you eat a bar the
yummy smell drifts under the
floorboards and into my room. I
can hardly bear it! I creep out
and watch you sitting on your
bed, munching away. I keep

hoping that you'll leave a tiny
piece for me. But you never do.
You eat every bit. You even
lick the wrapper . . . ! Oh, I'd do
anything to have a whole bar
of chocolate, all to myself."

Lucy thought about this for a few moments. Then she had an idea. "If I bought you a bar of chocolate, would you give me back some of my things?"

"A *whole* bar?" he asked.

"Of course."

"Yes! Yes! Yes!" The monster smiled and licked his lips.

"Great . . . !" cried Lucy, and
she gave him a list of what she
needed most, including, of
course, her new glasses. Then
Lucy had another, even better,
idea.

"How many bars of chocolate would it take for you to move *out* of my room and *into* somebody else's?" she asked, with a twinkle in her eye.

"Just one," replied the monster.

"But it would have to be one of those enormous giant-sized bars of thick milk chocolate with 144

squares! You know, like the one you had for your birthday. Give me a chocolate bar like that and I will move anywhere you like!"

"Then it's a deal!" laughed Lucy, and she shook his fat, wrinkly hand.

Chapter Four

That afternoon Lucy went to
the shops and spent her pocket
money on an enormous giant-
sized bar of thick milk chocolate
with 144 squares. Then, when

nobody was looking, she crept
up to her room and knocked
three times on the floor under
her bed. The Chocolate Monster
was waiting for her. And when
he saw the huge bar of
chocolate all three pairs of eyes
lit up!

"That's the one!" he cried and he gave her back everything she asked for. Then Lucy helped him pack his furniture and he moved out of her room for good.

Mum could hardly believe it when Lucy showed her all the things she had found: her silver ring, her lunchbox, her camera, the library books, two pairs of

gloves and all three pairs of
glasses.

"Where on earth did you find
them?" asked Mum.

"Under my bed," said Lucy

quite truthfully. And after she made her deal with the Chocolate Monster Lucy never lost a thing.

But Matthew started to lose *everything*! He couldn't understand what was happening. He lost his pencil case and one of his shin-pads. He lost his school reading book and his

new waterproof watch. He lost the top of his

pyjamas and the bottom of his tracksuit. He lost three footballs in a fortnight and two pairs of swimming trunks in a week. And then Mum really lost her temper.

"What's wrong with you,
Matthew?" she shouted. "You've
become so careless!"

"Why are you always losing
things?" added Dad crossly.
"Lucy never loses anything."

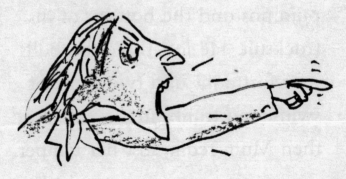

"I *don't* lose things," Matthew shouted back. "They just disappear!"

Lucy didn't tease him or sing nursery rhymes about people losing their pockets. She just followed him round the house, with a smug smile on her face.

And every so often – *when he wasn't being nasty to her* – she would creep up to his bedroom with a big bar of chocolate.

"Here we are, Matthew," she would say later. "I found these

things under your bed." And she would give him back just a few of the things he had lost.

"Thank you," Matthew would grunt back. And he never called her Lucy Locket again.

THE END